What do lizards do?

An Ivy and Mack story

T0337090

Written by Rebecca Colby
Illustrated by Gustavo Mazali

Collins

Who's in this story?

Listen and say

Download the audio at www.collins.co.uk/839675

Pete's Pet Shop

Alex's dad

Mack

Croc

Alex

🎧 Mack and his friend, Alex, are at the pet shop.

Alex's dad says, "Let's buy a pet."

Mack says, "What pet do you want, Alex?"

Mack looks at Alex.
"What do lizards do?"

Mack says, "Look at the fish. They swim."

Lizards swim.

Mack says, "Ahh! Listen! The hamsters are squeaking."

Mack says, "Rabbits hop!
Can lizards hop?"

Alex says, "No, they can't.
But they can climb."

Oh!

Mack says, "What about this mouse?
It is climbing. Look!"

10

Mack says, "Would you like a mouse, Alex?"

Alex says, "No, mice are too small."

Mack says, "Wow!"

Alex says, "Snakes are nice, but they don't have legs. Lizards have legs."

Alex sees a green lizard. He says,
"Look at this one. It has a long tail."

Mack says, "Is it sleeping?"

No.

The lizard does not move.
Mack asks, "Is it sad?"

No.

Mack says, "Alex, the lizard *isn't* climbing or swimming."

No, it isn't.

Alex's dad says, "Would you like the lizard, Alex?"

Alex says, "Yes please, Dad."

18

Alex gets his lizard.

Mack asks again, "What do lizards *do*?"

Alex says, "Lizards swim and climb and run! ... What does Croc do?"

Mack thinks.

Mack says, "I don't know!
But I like him."

Alex looks at Mack. "And I like
my lizard!"

Picture dictionary

Listen and repeat

climb

fish

hamster

lizard

mouse

pet shop

rabbit

snake

1 Look and order the story

2 Listen and say

Collins

Published by Collins
An imprint of HarperCollins*Publishers*
Westerhill Road
Bishopbriggs
Glasgow
G64 2QT

HarperCollins*Publishers*
1st Floor, Watermarque Building
Ringsend Road
Dublin 4
Ireland

William Collins' dream of knowledge for all began with the publication of his first book in 1819.

A self-educated mill worker, he not only enriched millions of lives, but also founded a flourishing publishing house. Today, staying true to this spirit, Collins books are packed with inspiration, innovation and practical expertise. They place you at the centre of a world of possibility and give you exactly what you need to explore it.

© HarperCollins*Publishers* Limited 2020

10 9 8 7 6 5 4 3 2

ISBN 978-0-00-839675-6

Collins® and COBUILD® are registered trademarks of HarperCollins*Publishers* Limited

www.collins.co.uk/elt

British Library Cataloguing in Publication Data

A catalogue record for this publication is available from the British Library.

Author: Rebecca Colby
Illustrator: Gustavo Mazali (Beehive)
Series editor: Rebecca Adlard
Publishing manager: Lisa Todd
Product managers: Jennifer Hall and Caroline Green
In-house editor: Alma Puts Keren
Project manager: Emily Hooton
Editor: Deborah Friedland
Proofreaders: Natalie Murray and Michael Lamb
Cover designer: Kevin Robbins
Typesetter: 2Hoots Publishing Services Ltd
Audio produced by id audio, London
Reading guide author: Julie Penn
Production controller: Rachel Weaver
Printed and bound by: GPS Group, Slovenia

MIX
Paper from
responsible sources

FSC C007454

Download the audio for this book and a reading guide for parents and teachers at www.collins.co.uk/839675